NODDY™

Makes a New Friend

HarperEntertainment
An Imprint of HarperCollinsPublishers

It was a quiet day in Toyland. Noddy was feeling a bit bored and was looking for something exciting to do.

As he drove into town, he saw that Mr. Plod had blocked the street with a line of traffic cones.

"I put these here," said Mr. Plod, pointing to the cones, "so I could direct the caravan from Binks's circus away from the center of town."

"A circus!" cried Noddy. "That's exciting. May I follow it?"

"If you want to," said Mr. Plod. In a hurry, Noddy drove straight through the line of cones, sending them all skidding across the street.

Farther down the road, Noddy came across a funny-looking creature sitting under a tree. The creature was moaning and clutching his foot.

"What are you?" asked Noddy. "Are you traveling with the circus?"

"I am a Bunkey," said the strange animal. "Half bunny and half monkey. Can't you see my rabbit ears? I fell off the circus caravan and hurt my leg. Ow!"

"Well, I could drive after the circus and help you get back into your caravan," said Noddy.

"Oh no, I don't want to go back to the circus, please!" cried the Bunkey. "I like it much better out here."

"Poor Bunkey," said Noddy. "You can stay at my house until your leg gets better."

"Oh, thank you," said the Bunkey gratefully.

He climbed into Noddy's car, and the two new friends returned to Toy Town, almost knocking poor Mr. Plod over on the way.

Back at Noddy's house, Noddy and the Bunkey were enjoying a cup of cocoa together.

"I really like your house, Noddy," said the Bunkey. "I can sleep in this cozy chair and when my leg is better, I'll clean your house from top to bottom, cook your dinner, wash and polish your car, weed your garden, and do your shopping, too!"

"Good gracious! What will *I* do then?" Noddy chuckled.

"Oh, please!" said the Bunkey. "I want to repay you for your kindness!"

"All right then, if you really want to," said Noddy.

Keeping his word, the Bunkey cleaned and polished Noddy's car until it shined brightly.

"I've never seen my car gleam like that, Bunkey!" said Noddy. "Thank you."

When Tessie Bear came to ask Noddy if he would drive her into town, Noddy introduced her to his new friend.

"Noddy has been so kind to me that I want to do whatever I can to help him," said the Bunkey. "If you are his friend, then I want to help you, too. Whenever you want anything at all, just tell me, and I'll try to do it for you."

"Well," said Tessie Bear, getting into Noddy's car, "I often wish we had a streetlight outside our house. Every night Uncle Bear bumps into the tree by our front gate, and wakes us all up when he cries, 'Ouch!'"

Noddy and Tessie Bear drove away, leaving the Bunkey looking thoughtful.

That night the Bunkey crept into Noddy's front yard and whistled. The garage door opened and out came Noddy's car. The Bunkey climbed in and quickly drove out of the driveway.

The next morning at breakfast the Bunkey kept yawning.

"Are you tired?" Noddy asked.

"No," said the Bunkey. "I'm just practicing opening my mouth so I can put this tasty boiled egg inside."

Just then Mr. Plod barged in and marched straight up to Noddy.

"Noddy," he demanded, "do you know anything about four missing streetlights? One was taken from outside Miss Pink Cat's house last night. The other was taken from outside my house—and we both heard the noise of a car. . . ."

"Well, it wasn't my car!" said Noddy. "Now if you don't mind, we are trying to eat breakfast."

"Yes, please go away!" said the Bunkey, jumping up.

Just then Tessie Bear came in. "There are four streetlights in our front yard! Where did . . . oh, hello, Mr. Plod."

"So that's where they've gone," said Mr. Plod. "Noddy, you'll be hearing from me again!" he added as he left.

"Bunkey," said Noddy sternly, "those streetlights, surely you didn't . . ."

"Oh dear, look at the time! I've got to weed the garden," said the Bunkey, rushing out the door.

"He must have done it. Oh dear!" said Noddy, holding his head in his hands.

Noddy and Tessie Bear followed the Bunkey into the garden and found him busily pulling up weeds.

"Bunkey, you must tell the truth," begged Noddy.

"Look out, Noddy!" Tessie Bear shouted. "Here comes Bumpy Dog! You know how excited he gets when he sees you!"

Bumpy Dog ran up and licked Noddy's face with glee.

"Oh, please stop it, Bumpy Dog!" said Noddy, petting him.

But just then a weed came flying through the air, landing right on Bumpy Dog's nose.

"Go away!" said the Bunkey. "How dare you attack my friend Noddy."

He rushed at Bumpy Dog to shoo him away, but Bumpy Dog just knocked the Bunkey over and licked *his* face, too.

The Bunkey and Bumpy Dog chased each other all over Noddy's garden. At last, too tired to go on, they collapsed on the bench, breaking it into tiny pieces.

"You silly dog!" said Noddy. "You've ruined my garden. And you are just as silly, Bunkey!"

"I'm sorry," said the Bunkey. "I only wanted to protect you. I'll put your garden back to the way it was, I promise."

Later that day Noddy and Tessie Bear returned to find that the garden had been replanted with new flowers and that the bench had been replaced, too.

"It's that Bunkey again!" cried Noddy. "That's not a *garden* bench, it's a *park* bench! Bunkey, come here!"

The Bunkey crept out from behind the park bench.

"I didn't steal them!" he pleaded. "I asked a park gardener, 'Who owns this bench and these flowers?' He said, 'They belong to everyone.' That means they're yours, too, so I brought them home for you."

"Oh, you've done a very silly thing, Bunkey!" said Noddy. "You'd better come with me to the police station and tell them it was *you* who took the streetlights and the park bench."

"No, I don't want to!" cried the Bunkey.

At the police station Noddy nudged the Bunkey in front of Mr. Plod.

"Bunkey has come to say he's very sorry for taking the streetlights and park bench. . . ."

"Bunkey?" said Mr. Plod, pulling off the Bunkey's hat. "There's no such thing as a Bunkey. See? These ears are sewn onto his hat. He's just a monkey! I got a letter from the circus warning me about him. They had to let him go because they'd had enough of his naughty tricks."

"But you told me you'd fallen out of the caravan," said Noddy. "Oh, Bunkey, how could you. . . ."

But the Bunkey was already outside climbing into Noddy's car.

"I'm sorry, Noddy," he called as he drove off. "I just wanted to be your friend."

Noddy and Tessie Bear walked home sadly.

"I really miss my car. Will I ever see it again?" wondered Noddy.

Just then they heard a *beep! beep!*

"My car!" cried Noddy. "Bunkey sent it back! Maybe he was my friend after all."

"He must have just borrowed it to get away because he was so frightened of Mr. Plod," said Tessie Bear.

"He wasn't really a Bunkey, but I liked him anyway," Tessie Bear added.

"I liked him, too," said Noddy. "He did always try to do the right thing, you know. I just wonder if he's found a new disguise!"

Laughing, Noddy and Tessie Bear went into the house, and neither of them even noticed the strange animal dancing on the garage roof, which was probably just as well.

READ AND LEARN FROM MORE DELIGHTFUL NODDY BOOKS

Noddy Meets Santa
Noddy Gives a Birthday Party

NODDY MAKES A NEW FRIEND
Originally published in the United Kingdom in 1995 by BBC Children's Books
First U.S. edition published by HarperEntertainment in 2000
Text, design, and stills copyright © 1995
Enid Blyton Limited and BBC Worldwide Limited. All rights reserved.
No part of this book may be used or reproduced in any manner whatsoever
without written permission of the publishers.
For information address HarperCollins Publishers Inc.,
10 East 53rd Street, New York, NY 10022-5299.

Copyrights are the property of Enid Blyton Limited/BBC Worldwide Limited (All rights reserved). Trademarks
are the property of Enid Blyton Limited (All rights reserved). Licensed by the itsy bitsy Entertainment Company.

Based on the television series *Noddy*, a BBC Worldwide Ltd/Enid Blyton Ltd/Catalyst Entertainment Inc.
co-production. Original animated series produced by Cosgrove Hall Films, based on the books by Enid Blyton.

ISBN 0-06-107367-9
HarperCollins®, 🏭®, and HarperEntertainment™ are trademarks of HarperCollins Publishers Inc.
Printed in the United States
Visit HarperEntertainment on the World Wide Web at www.harpercollins.com